THE GENIE IN THE JAR

THE GENIE IN THE JAR

NIKKI GIOVANNI

ILLUSTRATED BY CHRIS RASCHKA

HENRY HOLT AND COMPANY   NEW YORK

for Nina Simone

—N.G.

for Ingo

—C.R.

Henry Holt and Company, Inc., *Publishers since 1866*
115 West 18th Street, New York, New York 10011
Henry Holt is a registered trademark
of Henry Holt and Company, Inc.
Text copyright © 1996 by Nikki Giovanni
Illustrations copyright © 1996 by Chris Raschka
All rights reserved.
Published in Canada by Fitzhenry & Whiteside Ltd.,
195 Allstate Parkway, Markham, Ontario L3R 4T8.

Library of Congress Cataloging-in-Publication Data
Giovanni, Nikki.
The genie in the jar / by Nikki Giovanni ;
illustrated by Chris Raschka.
Summary: In this hymn to the power of art and of love,
the words create images of black songs and black loom, inspiring
readers to trust their hearts.
1. Afro-Americans—Juvenile poetry. 2. Children's poetry, American.
[1. Afro-Americans—Poetry. 2. American poetry.]
I. Raschka, Christopher, ill. II. Title.
PS3557.I55G46 1996 811'.54—dc20   95-23503

ISBN 0-8050-4118-4 First Edition—1996
Printed in the United States of America on acid-free paper. ∞
10 9 8 7 6 5 4 3 2 1

The artist used india ink, oil sticks, and watercolor
on Fabriano Ingres paper to create the illustrations for this book.

take a note

and spin it around

spin it around

don't

prick your finger

take a note

and spin it around

on the Black loom

on the Black loom

careful baby

don't prick your finger

take the air

and weave the sky

around the Black loom

around the Black loom

make the sky sing a Black song
sing a blue song

sing my song make the sky
sing a Black song

from the Black loom from the Black loom

careful baby

don't prick your finger

take a genie

and put her in a jar

put her in a jar
wrap the sky around her

take the genie and put her in a jar
wrap the sky around her

listen to her sing
sing a Black song our Black song
from the Black loom

singing to me
from the Black loom

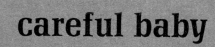

careful baby

don't prick your finger